Moo to Poo

potty training for toddlers

(it isn't just for kids!)

By Ellen Ostroth

-PRESS-

Written by Ellen Ostroth

Technical design by Thane Ostroth

JMND Press

Moo to Moo©Ellen Ostroth2020

All rights reserved-no parts may be reproduced without permission and licensing.

First edition: September 2020

Forward

The hardest part of potty training can be pooping in the potty.

***Never fear!* Momma Cow has a plan.**

Moo to Poo is a fun look at taking the frustration out of potty training. *Works wonders for constipated or struggling "kids of all ages."*

Acknowledgments

Moo to Poo, as a potty-training children's book has been a pleasure to create. I understand the concept originated in Australia. The idea behind <u>Moo to Poo</u> is to say "moo" out loud. Several times, if needed. At the same time, it may be helpful to wriggle your seated body sideways, and back and forth. Mooing engages the correct muscles for "pushing" or eliminating. Any resistant muscles are overcome and forced to work correctly.

I thank Christine Green, DPT, a wonderful pelvic floor specialist, who shared this technique with me. I told her I should write a book and we laughed and laughed. And yet here it is!

Many thanks, Dr. Green, from many of us. (Yes, it works for constipated people of all ages!)

This book was tested out on my 2 ½-year-old granddaughter Aislin, who giggled wildly throughout the pages. Thanks honey.

I do believe that's a "thumbs up!"

Momma Cow went for a walk.

"Why do you look so mad?" Momma Cow asked baby duck.

"Because I keep trying, but I can't poop in my potty!"

"Moo," said Mama Cow. "*Mo-o-o-o-o* to poo."

Baby duck giggled but said, "*M-o-o-o-o*!"

PLOP!

"It worked!"

Momma Cow nodded and walked on.

She came across baby lamb.

"Why do you look so sad?"

"I can't poop in my potty, and my mommy wants me to."

Baby lamb sighed.

"You have to say *'m-o-o-o-o'* to poo," said Momma Cow.

"Moo is for cows. I'm a lamb!"

"*M-o-o-o-o* helps everyone to poo."

Momma Cow was smiling because she knew!

"Okay. Um...*m-o-o-o-o! M-o-o-o!*"

PLOP!

Baby lamb laughed.

Mommy is so proud of me!"

Momma Cow smiled and walked on.

Soon Momma Cow found baby pig.

"What is wrong?"

"I'm bored," said baby pig.

"Mommy and Daddy say I have to poop in the potty, but it takes too long."

"Wiggle back and forth a little and say *M-o-o-o-o-o*!"

Momma Cow winked.

Baby pig got the wiggle-giggles but did as Momma Cow had suggested.

PLOP!

"That was fast and easy!"

"Yes! You have to 'm-o-o-o-o-o' to poo."

"Thank you, Momma Cow," said Mommy Pig.

Momma Cow went on until she spied baby chick.

"Why are you crying?"

"I want to go play, but Daddy says I have to sit on my potty until I poop."

"You have to 'm-o-o-o-o' to poo," replied Momma Cow.

Baby chick crossed her eyes and grunted.

"M-o-o-o-o-o-o-o-o!"

Plop! Plop! Plop!

"That was so easy! I can poop on the potty."

Baby chick was excited.

Momma Cow made her way back to the barn.

Baby calf was waiting for her.

"I pooped in my potty!"

Baby calf was smiling.

"Of course you did, dear. You know the secret!"

"**M-o-o-o-o** to poo!" said baby calf.

Momma Cow was very happy.

"Can you '*m-o-o-o-o*' to poo?"

The End.

About the Author

Ellen's other books include: Elandra, the Spiritual Warrior trilogy series: The Art of Beauty; The Art of Betrayal; The Art of Being; and The Art of Bravery now at Amazon.com. Other new books include "Mommy and Daddy Are Getting a Divorce...Now What?" and "The How to Thrive Book" – Shamanic Techniques for the for Lay Person, co-authored with her husband Thane.

Ellen & Thane are currently working on a Level II shamanic book intended for energy practitioners. Also look for Ellen's book of short stories coming soon.

You can also read Ellen's blogs on www.stonewisdom.net. Ellen is on Instagram.com. and Facebook. Don't forget to check out the family-friendly Divine Whisperings on YouTube.com, promoting sleep and self-confidence.

Thane & Ellen Ostroth can be reached at stonewisdom555@yahoo.com.

Made in the USA
Columbia, SC
12 September 2020